BO(

Wr

Their Eyes Were Watching God

BY ZORA NEALE HURSTON

BrightSummaries.com

ZORA NEALE HURSTON

AMERICAN WRITER

- **Born in Notasulga, Alabama in 1891.**
- **Died in Fort Pierce, Florida in 1960.**
- **Notable works:**
    - *Mules and Men* (1935), a study of African-American folklore
    - *Moses, Man of the Mountain* (1939), novel
    - *Dust Tracks on a Road* (1942), autobiography

Zora Neale Hurston was an African-American writer and folklorist who can be linked with the Harlem Renaissance, a period of blossoming of African-American arts and culture which took place mainly in Harlem, New York (c. 1918-1937). This movement was very significant for the development of African-American literature.

Hurston grew up in Eatonville, Florida, which was one of the first all-black towns in the United States. She experienced poverty and difficulties in her life, but she managed to study anthropology, explore African-American language and culture and write fiction and non-fiction. Although she was a successful writer in her time, by the end of 1950s she was 'forgotten' and working as a maid. The true recognition of her talent and the importance of her works came posthumously. She is now considered to have been one of the most important African-American writers of the 20th century. Many contemporary African-American female writers, such as Alice Walker and Toni Morrison, consider her to be their literary foremother.

Hurston explores African-American culture, folklore and language in her writing, and uses her personal experiences and her anthropological knowledge to bring African-American culture to life in her fiction.

THEIR EYES WERE WATCHING GOD

AN AFRICAN-AMERICAN FOLK ROMANCE

- **Genre:** novel
- **Reference edition:** Hurston, Z. N. (2007) *Their Eyes Were Watching God*. London: Virago Press.
- **1st edition:** 1937
- **Themes:** love, female empowerment, independence, language and speech, African-American culture

Their Eyes Were Watching God can be described as a folk romance. It is the story of Janie, an African-American woman who searches for love, happiness and emancipation. She gets married three times, but finds love and fulfilment only in her last marriage. Love and women's place in love relationships are central to the novel. Although love is the driving force of Janie's story, her need to be free to make her own choices and the way she learns to use her own voice are equally important.

The characters in the novel are African-American, and their cultural identity and language are integral parts of the novel. Hurston uses African-American Vernacular English to give her characters authentic voices, and the dialogue is representative of African-American culture in the early 20th century. Hurston both grew up in the culture which she describes and studied it as an anthropologist. This makes the language use and the representation of the characters, their culture and the novel's setting rich, believable and meaningful.

SUMMARY

JANIE BEGINS HER STORY

The novel opens with Janie, a middle-aged woman, coming back home to Eatonville after a long absence under the watchful eyes of her neighbours. Janie had left Eatonville with a younger man and the neighbours are gossiping about what could have happened to her after she left, and whether the young man had left Janie and took her money. Janie's best friend, Pheoby, goes to greet Janie and to find out what has happened. Janie explains everything to Pheoby, starting from her childhood experiences.

Janie was brought up by Nanny, her grandmother. Nanny had been a slave before slavery was abolished. Janie's mother was conceived when Nanny was abused by her slave master, and after the birth of her baby, Nanny escaped the anger of his jealous wife. She found work, now as a free person since slavery had ended, with a white family. Janie's mother too was raped (in her case by her teacher), and she disappeared from Janie's life soon after giving birth to her. Because of these experiences, when Nanny sees Janie kissing a local boy, she decides to marry her off so that she can have a better life and a more secure status than her mother and grandmother had had.

Janie marries Logan Killicks, an older man who owns a great deal of land. Janie does not love him, and feels unhappy with him. She had dreamed of love and fulfilment in marriage but does not find it with her husband. Nanny thinks that Janie should be pleased with what she has, but she is distressed by Janie's unhappiness. She dies soon after hearing about her granddaughter's disappointment with her marriage.

EATONVILLE

One day Janie meets Joe Stark, a charismatic man who plans to go to Eatonville and become someone important there. After several meetings, Janie decides to run away with him. Janie and Joe get married and move to Eatonville, where Joe buys land and becomes a landlord, store owner and the mayor. Janie, who is considered to be very attractive, discovers that Joe wanted her as a possession he is proud to show off, and not as a partner. While Janie is materially comfortable and Joe holds her superior to other women in town, she is not content. She would like to participate more in the town's life, but Joe thinks she should hold herself apart because of her status as his wife. Joe controls Janie's life, which makes her unhappy, but for years she obeys her husband. Janie observes life in Eatonville, and especially enjoys the conversations which take place on the porch of the store. She would like to take part in the conversations, but Joe does not allow this. One recurrent topic of conversation is Matt Boner's mule. Many imaginative stories featuring the mule, who is stubborn and, according to the townspeople, not very well fed, are told on the porch. One day, after Joe hears Janie saying to herself that the people should be ashamed of themselves for the way they tease the mistreated animal, he buys the mule from Matt Boner, so that it can be free. The free mule becomes a topic of stories and conversation, and an important part of the life of the people in Eatonville until it dies.

After years of silently bending to her husband's will and letting him criticise her whenever he wants to, one day, when Joe criticises Janie over her looks and reminds her that, at almost 40, she is no longer a young girl, she answers back and tells him that he is over 50, and that it shows too. This happens in the store, in front of many people. Joe is furious and hits Janie. After this, their marriage is changed forever. They continue to live together as a married couple, but avoid contact with one another. Soon after this, Joe becomes ill and dies. Before his death, Janie tells him he never allowed her to live as she wanted to.

JANIE FINDS HAPPINESS WITH TEA CAKE

After Joe's death, many men express interest in Janie, but she enjoys her freedom. She does not want to marry someone to secure her status or for any other practical reasons. Janie does not show any interest in men until she falls in love with Tea Cake, a man in his twenties who seems to be interested in her because of her beauty and her personality rather than because of her wealth and her status. Janie and Tea Cake decide to get married and leave Eatonville. People in

Eatonville do not approve of Janie and Tea Cake's relationship because of their age gap, and because Tea Cake is not wealthy like Janie. Pheoby warns Janie that Tea Cake might be after her money, but Janie trusts him.

Tea Cake proves to be worthy of Janie's trust. Although he disappears for a night as he goes out with Janie's money that he found, and spends some of it, he comes back to Janie and promises to repay her once he has won some by gambling. Janie is upset because he did not take her with him, and he promises that in future he will ask her to join him. Tea Cake also tells Janie to keep the money she has in the bank and that they will live on the money that he earns.

Tea Cake and Janie go to the Everglades and work picking up beans. Janie is happy with her life working side by side with Tea Cake and with the friends they have. Although their relationship has its problems, such as both of them getting jealous sometimes, they are happy together. Janie and Tea Cake love and respect each other, and Janie feels she has found the fulfilment she did not find in her previous marriages.

Janie's happiness with Tea Cake comes to an end when they are caught up in a storm and Tea Cake gets bitten by a rabid dog when saving Janie from drowning. Tea Cake and Janie do not realise right away that the dog has rabies, but three weeks later Tea Cake becomes very ill. Janie tries to care for him, but she is eventually forced to shoot him to save her own life when he becomes dangerous in a fit of rage caused by his illness. Janie is put on trial, but found not guilty of murdering him.

Janie organises a lavish funeral for Tea Cake, which their friends attend. Although Tea Cake's friends were angry at Janie for shooting him at first, they end up admitting that they know she loved him and understand why she had to do it. They ask Janie to stay in the Everglades, but she only stays for a few weeks because she cannot bear being there without Tea Cake.

RETURN TO EATONVILLE

Janie returns to Eatonville. The narration returns to where it started, with Janie and Pheoby talking after Janie's return. Pheoby is impressed by what Janie has told her. Pheoby goes home, leaving Janie alone in her house. That night Janie feels Tea Cake's presence and feels at peace in the company of his memory.

CHARACTER STUDY

JANIE

Janie is a passionate, attractive and intelligent woman. She is of mixed race, but does not want to set herself 'above' the black community as another mixed-raced character does.

Janie searches for true love and emancipation. As a young girl, she experienced bliss when watching bees pollinating a pear tree (pp. 14-15), and she seeks this bliss in love. She gets married three times, but does not find fulfilment in her first two marriages because these two men do not seek this type of bliss. Janie does not feel sufficiently loved or heard in these two marriages. She only finds happiness in marriage when she marries a man who loves her as she is, and who wants to hear what she has to say. Janie also enjoys her freedom after the death of her second husband, which shows that she does not need a man to feel content. This is important for her emancipation. It is also significant that she begins to find her own voice before she meets Tea Cake, when she finally stands up for herself against her second husband. This means that although Tea Cake helps her in becoming her true self, she is the author of her own emancipation. In fact, she finds bliss with Tea Cake because he respects her and allows her to express her personality.

TEA CAKE

Tea Cake is Janie's third husband. He is happy, sociable and likable. However, people in Janie's community do not approve of Janie and Tea Cake's relationship because he is much younger than Janie, and because he works odd jobs and gambles. Many people believe that he is only interested in her money, but he loves her for who she is. Janie finds the love she has been dreaming of since she was a young girl with him. He respects her and encourages her to express herself and to try new things. For example, he teaches her to shoot (which also means that he is the one who teaches Janie the skill she later needs to defend herself against him when he is violent because of his illness). Janie and Tea Cake do everything together, but he does not expect her to change herself for him, nor does she depend on him any more than he depends on her. While Janie and Tea Cake's relationship is not perfect because of problems such as jealousy, it is a relationship based on love and mutual respect.

JOE STARKS

Joe Starks is Janie's second husband. He is an ambitious man who wants to be a "big ruler of things" (p. 39). He becomes a landlord, a store owner and the mayor in Eatonville, thus fulfilling his aspirations. He is respected in his community, but Janie is not happy with him. Janie too seems to be a part of his ambitious plans: he treats her like a precious possession to be proud of, and not like a partner. He provides for Janie, but expects her to obey him, and does not let her have a will of her own. He has deeply sexist ideas about women and marriage, as he does not think that Janie can think for herself. He says: "Somebody got to think for women and chillun and chickens and cows. I, god, they sho don't think none theirselves" (p. 95). Joe also openly criticises Janie, and when she finally answers back, their marriage practically ends, even though they stay married and live together until he dies. Janie only finds freedom after his death.

PHEOBY WATSON

Pheoby is Janie's best friend. The two women have been friends for 20 years. When Janie comes back to Eatonville after having been away with Tea Cake, Pheoby defends her friend against gossiping townspeople and goes to welcome her home and find out what has happened. Janie tells her story to Pheoby, who is impressed by what she hears. Before Janie left, Pheoby had warned Janie that Tea Cake might be after her money, but she respected Janie's decision. Now, she is happy to hear that Janie had found happiness with Tea Cake.

NANNY

Nanny is Janie's grandmother. She has experienced slavery, racism and sexism. She had Janie's mother as a result of being raped by her slave master, and then escaped his jealous wife. After slavery was abolished, she found work with a white family. The white people she works for now are kind, but this type of work means that she remains in the service of white people. Nanny hopes for a better life first for her daughter, and then for her granddaughter when this fails. Nanny's daughter, Leafy, is raped too, and she too has her rapist's child. Leafy starts to drink and to stay out soon after Janie's birth, and eventually disappears from Janie's life. Nanny puts all her hopes in securing the future of her granddaughter. When she sees Janie kissing a local boy, she wants to marry Janie off as quickly as possible in order to secure her future. She does not think that there are many options for black women in America. She tells Janie that "De nigger woman is de mule uh de world" (p. 19). This is why she thinks that marrying a wealthy man is the best thing for her granddaughter. Although Janie suffers as a result of Nanny's determination to have her married, her intentions are good. Nanny's worldview is coloured by her experiences. Nanny becomes very sad when she realises that Janie is unhappy in her marriage.

LOGAN KILLICKS

Logan Killicks is Janie's first husband. He is wealthy, and Nanny wants Janie to marry him to obtain a better social status and security, which is something that Nanny herself never had.

However, Janie is unhappy with him. He is much older than her, unattractive and unromantic. He wants a practical marriage and for Janie to help him with his work. Janie does not feel in love or loved, and eventually runs away with Joe Starks.

ANALYSIS

AN AFRICAN-AMERICAN FOLK ROMANCE

Their Eyes Were Watching God examines African-American culture. Its two main areas of focus are love relationships, primarily the one between Janie and Tea Cake, and black folk culture in the Southern United Sates. The novel's main purpose is not to explore black people as victims of white racism – although it is far from absent from the lives of the novel's characters – but to celebrate and explore black culture in its own right. Most of the novel's characters are black, and a large part of the novel is set in the all-black town of Eatonville. Hurston's novel explores race in America by focusing on African-American culture and language, which gives ordinary Southern African-Americans voices. This is as important as exposing white racism. Dubey maintains that Hurston chooses to portray African-American life by "exploring its cultural vitality and its internal conflicts of colour, class and gender rather than its dehumanizing confrontation with white racism" (Dubey, 2009: 158).

Hurston is able to write about black folk culture in a meaningful way because, as Wall has remarked, her experience of growing up in an all-black town and her training in anthropology "deepened her appreciation for and understanding of the culture of the rural blacks" (Wall, 2009: 44). She makes her prose rich and expressive by including many characters with different personalities who discuss a range of subjects with each other and tell each other stories. Joe Starks's store's porch, for example, provides an ideal setting for these exchanges. One good example of the conversations on the porch is the 'mule talk'. The townspeople tell elaborate stories of what the mule, which first belonged to Matt Bonner and was later 'freed' by Joe Starks, has done. These conversations show imagination and enjoyment in storytelling, and they are examples of creative use of language. Other examples include the playful way in which men talk to women who are considered to be attractive: ""Gal Ah'm crazy 'bout you", Charlie goes on to the entertainment of everybody. "Ah'll do anything in the world except work for you and give you mah money'"' (p. 90). These, and many other conversations in the novel illustrate and celebrate black American folk culture. Hurston also uses African-American Vernacular English (AAVE) as part of her exploration of black American culture.

THE LEGACY OF SLAVERY AND THE AFRICAN-AMERICAN EXPERIENCE IN THE 20TH CENTURY

While the novel primarily focuses on exploring African-American life rather than on racism, racism does nevertheless feature in the novel. As *Their Eyes Were Watching God* was published in 1937 and is set in the United States of this era (and earlier), the African-Americans in the novel are subjected to institutional racism. White racism is present in the novel, as it is present in the lives of black people, especially in this era. The most obvious example of racial injustice in the novel is Nanny's slave narrative. Nanny was treated like property, used as forced labour and sexually exploited by her slave master. She did not get any more sympathy from her mistress, who instead of feeling empathy towards Nanny, who was raped, reacted with jealous anger towards her (pp. 23-24). Nanny's past as a slave, her rape, and the rape of her daughter impact her for the rest of her life, and by extension Janie's life. Even after the end of slavery, black people were considered as second-class citizens. All the characters in the novel live under racial oppression. Nanny says that "de white man is de ruler of everything" (p. 19), and this is the unfair reality for the characters in the novel, and for the author of the book. Hurston's folk romance that celebrates African-American culture can therefore be seen as an act of empowerment, against racism.

FEMALE EMANCIPATION

In addition to racism, the novel's female characters experience sexism. Nanny's sexual exploitation is an example of both racism and sexism. Tasharofi and Afrougheh explain that "the female slave lived in constant awareness of her sexual vulnerability that any male, white or Black, might assault her" (Tasharofi & Afrougheh, 2014: 753). Since Nanny has faced violent oppression and abuse because of her race and her gender, it is easy to understand why she would think that Janie would need to marry a man like Logan Killicks for protection. This, however, means keeping Janie subjugated to male authority. Janie, on the other hand, does not intend to stay in this position, as she runs away from him. Unfortunately, Joe Starks does not mean the end of male oppression for her. For years she remains passive and obedient to her authoritative husband, until one day, she finally answers back when he criticises her and reminds her that she is ageing: "Yeah, Ah'm nearly forty and you'se already fifty. How come you can't talk about dat sometimes instead of always pointin' at me?" (p. 106). This marks the end of their relationship as they know it even though they stay married until he dies. After's Joe's death, Janie does not seek a man, but enjoys her freedom. This is another step forward on her way to empowerment. When she does begin a relationship, she does it out of love, of her own free will, and with a man who respects her and encourages her to find her own voice.

A LOVE STORY

Janie finds fulfilment with Tea Cake, and the love they share is an important part of the novel. Not only does Tea Cake help Janie along on her way towards empowerment, but she discovers the love she dreamed of in her youth with him. Janie's vision of a bee pollinating a pear tree is the symbol of her sexual awakening, and a romantic vison of relationships between men and women. Janie is disappointed in her first two marriages, but finally finds this romantic, blissful love with Tea Cake. Their relationship has its ups and downs, but because it is based on mutual respect and the will to make one another happy, it is strong. Janie's and Tea Cake's love story is contrasted with Janie's previous relationships. Tea Cake does not offer Janie wealth and status like her previous husbands did. Instead, he offers her his affection, his time, his company and his devotion. Unlike Logan and Joe, Tea Cake teaches Janie to do things she might enjoy, such as playing games, fishing and shooting, and, importantly, he enjoys spending time with her. Moreover, Tea Cake wants Janie to work with him, not because he wants her help, but because he wants her close to him. He tells Janie: "Ah gits lonesome out dere all day 'thout yuh" (p. 178). Janie and Tea Cake's happiness comes to a tragic end when Tea Cake becomes ill with rabies and Janie is forced to shoot him to protect herself. However, Janie finds peace in the end by keeping his memory close to her heart.

STYLE

Their Eyes Were Watching God is stylistically remarkable. The most important stylistic elements include poetic language and metaphors, the use of AAVE and a third person omniscient narrator, with some passages in free indirect discourse.

The omniscient third person narrator can provide the reader with information on the thoughts and experiences of different characters. This is significant because it allows the reader to know more than any of the characters in the novel. For example, when Janie finally answers back to Joe when he criticises her, the narrator conveys the feelings of both Janie and Joe to the reader. Hurston also uses free indirect discourse, which can be understood as a mix of first person and third person narration, to convey her characters' thoughts and feelings. This is used, for example, when describing Janie's feelings when she is observing the pear tree (pp. 14-15).

This passage is also a good example of poetic, symbolic use of language. This symbolic description of Janie's sexual awakening using the tree and the bees makes it beautiful and romantic and deepens the reader's understating of Janie's experiences.

LANGUAGE

The language used in *Their Eyes Were Watching God* is remarkable. Hurston uses grammatical structures typical of AAVE and respellings that convey the non-standard pronunciation of the characters in dialogue. She uses AAVE so extensively that it is one of the most noticeable features of the novel. As Hurston explores African-American culture in the novel, it is fitting that the language use reflects this. In fact, the language use in the novel extends beyond an ordinary stylistic device used to support the content, as the language used is a part of the content of the novel.

Barry (2001) demonstrates that Hurston uses the spelling and grammar of AAVE systematically and meaningfully throughout the novel. Hurston grew up speaking the variety of AAVE she uses in the novel, and she also studied it anthropologically. This means that she has the practical skills and the theoretical understanding necessary to use Southern African-American language as a tool to explore African-American folk culture.

Regarding grammar and spelling, observe, for example, the grammar and spelling of the following quote of Nanny speaking to Janie: "Ah ain't gittin ole, honey. Ah'm done ole" (p. 20). The use of the perfective "done" in this sentence is a good example of how Hurston uses grammatical structures that are representative of AAVE. Regarding spelling, the use of "Ah" instead of "I" in this quote shows how Hurston uses respellings in *Their Eyes Were Watching God* to illustrate AAVE pronunciation. Barry quotes Hurston's 1934 essay entitled "Characteristics of Negro Expression" to show that this a systematic, well thought out respelling. Hurston writes that "'Very few Negroes, educated or not, use a clear clipped "I". It verges more or less upon

"Ah"'" (Barry, 2001: 180). This example shows how Hurston wishes to accurately represent AAVE in her novel. The result is a clearly marked spelling and grammar (but not so marked that it would make the novel difficult to understand), which makes the novel seem authentic and deepens the exploration of its themes.

FURTHER REFLECTION

SOME QUESTIONS TO THINK ABOUT…

- Discuss Janie's three husbands and the differences between them. How do these relationships influence Janie?
- In your opinion, does Janie seek emancipation in love? Does she find it in her relationship with Tea Cake or in her independence?
- Discuss the symbolism connected with the freed mule in the novel.
- How would you interpret the novel's title?
- Discuss Nanny's experiences as a slave and how they influenced her relationship with her granddaughter.
- Discuss the language used in the novel. What is its impact?
- The porch of the store is an important place in the novel. Why do you think that is? What is its symbolic meaning?
- There are many minor characters in the novel. Discuss the differences and the similarities between them.

We want to hear from you!
Leave a comment on your online library
and share your favourite books on social media!

FURTHER READING

REFERENCE EDITION

- Hurston, Z. N. (2007) *Their Eyes Were Watching God*. London: Virago Press.

REFERENCE STUDIES

- Barry, B. (2001) "It's hard fuh me to understand what you mean, de way you tell it": representing language in Zora Neale Hurston's *Their Eyes Were Watching God*. *Language and Literature*. 10(2), pp. 171–186.
- Dubey, M. (2009) "Even some fiction might be useful": African America women novelists. In: A. Mitchell and D. K. Taylor eds., *The Cambridge Companion to African American Women's Literature*. Cambridge: Cambridge University Press, pp. 150-167.
- Tasharofi, P. and Afrougheh, S. (2014) Nanny's Slave Narrative in Zora Neale Hurston's *Their Eyes Were Watching God*: A Black Feminist Reading. *The Anthropologist*. 18(3), pp. 751-759.
- Wall, C. A. (2009) Women of the Harlem Renaissance. In A. Mitchell and D. K. Taylor eds.,

The Cambridge Companion to African American Women's Literature. Cambridge: Cambridge University Press, pp. 32-49.

ADAPTATIONS

- *Their Eyes Were Watching God*. (2005) [Film]. Darnell Martin. Dir. USA: American Broadcasting Company (ABC), Do We Inc., Harpo Films.

www.brightsummaries.com

Ebook EAN: 9782808016117

Paperback EAN: 9782808016124

Legal Deposit: D/2018/12603/566

Digital conception by Primento, the digital partner of publishers.

Printed in Great Britain
by Amazon

42583032R00032